# Free Agents
## Espionage On a College Campus

*A Syllble Studios Production*

**By**
**Vladimir Edouard**
**Elena Novak**
**Sam Luebbers**

Syllble Studios

Copyright © 2018 by Syllble, Inc.

All rights reserved.

# Table of Contents

# INTRODUCTION

In this small book we introduce you to a fictional world produced collaboratively. The following stories are vignettes from the characters lives. Snippets into their world. --

On the second floor of a hopelessly New Age brownstone in Washington, D.C, a neat, bespectacled man in his late twenties mindlessly paced his furnished bedroom. His very deep Russian features, though sullen, aloof, and plainly honorable, indicated a rotting nature brought to the limits of its endurance. An impassioned lecturer, one might have thought, noting the bookish forward lean and purpled eye bags and the entrenched brow. Certainly it would not have occurred to many people, even in their most conspiratorial dreams that he was an upper-ranking Soviet intelligence officer, hauled from his cherished desks in the annals of the Poetry (or Latin, or Shakespeare, or Physics) section in one of the more silent corridors of Lenin's State Library to be dispatched on a top-secret mission of absolute sensitivity.

While the world deals with the chaos of Bill Clinton's Monica Lewinsky scandal, a rouge Soviet spy must deal with the fallout of his pledging allegiance to a new country.

People grow jaded with the worlds they've built around themselves. They leave. Some would rate it more to be where they are from. But they will not go back. Ever. There is no hope where they are from. Here is better.

A Soviet intelligence officer is taught how to unlearn human feelings. While the rest of mankind is taught to play the victim, the Soviet intelligence officer is always in control. Always in control.

# MAIN CHARACTERS

## SARAH

Sarah, 31, works an administrative position in a mid-level think tank, recently re-enrolled at Georgetown University. She has received degrees in political science, public administration, and is working towards a masters in sociology. She is pretty, but only to those who know what they're looking for. She visits her parents often on weekends, and is in a budding relationship.

Sarah hides a deeper ambition behind her normal life, telling herself everyday that the path she is on is the one she has always wanted to take. She grew up with a desire to become a field officer in the FBI, but has long since put that dream aside for more attainable goals. Her routine is an escape from herself, and she is happy, so long as she continues to remind herself of such.

Sarah's motivation comes from her family. Her parents lived a very normal suburban life that they attest was very fulfilling. They came from a rural background, and moved to the closer to the city to allow Sarah to find more success than they ever could, and she feels that she owes it to them to do just that. On nights when she accidentally finds time to think about her life, she is reminded of the risks she always wanted to take, but they have remained just thoughts, and nothing more.

## VINNY

Vinny (not his real name) is Elias' handler. He parents were from western Europe, but moved to Russia when they became enthralled with the Marxist ideology. At his parent's behest, he joined the KGB at age 16, and has been an exemplary soldier of the motherland for 4 decades, but was often overlooked for promotions. He was a pleasant child, eager to make a name for himself, but his work, especially in recent years, has made him apathetic. To Elias, and other undisclosed members of his network, he is callous and routine, but they are unaware of his double life. 14 years ago, when he first came to America, a lapse in judgement with a woman he thought he loved brought forth a son. His health is currently uncertain at best.

Vinny has been living with the shame of his mistake for years, and the stress of keeping the knowledge of an illegitimate American son from his handlers has left him cold and unemotional. The child he once was is all but lost, and in the face of the collapse of the Soviet Union, his identity itself is likewise collapsing around him.

Vinny is motivated by his one mistake, and despite the events occurring in Russia, will not let himself be lax. He is determined to keep a firm hold on each of his spies, especially in this time of crisis, and sees this as his opportunity to prove himself, and be finally achieve something worth remembering.

## ELIAS

Elias is a Russian sleeper agent, 29 years old, plain-faced, shorter than the average but not to a point that anyone would take notice. He dresses, talks, and for all intents and purposes is a young intellectual, but he can't be sure if that is who he is, or because his cover demanded it so. He is a chameleon, someone who can blend into any social setting. His personality is therefore unstable, because up to this point in his life, it has always been assigned to him.

Elias is a soul torn between the old and new, between home and hope, between the past and the unknown. Elias finds himself at a crossroads in his life, and must choose to cling to what he knows or to abandon it all for the new life presented to him.

Elias desires to stand out. But first, he must understand who he is, a difficult task, when he has been trained to live inside another person's life for as long as he can remember. He has been a spy for so long, that with this new opportunity, he's not sure he knows how to live. He longs for real human connection

# Sarah Palmer: Vignette 1

"When are you going to spend the money you've earned your whole life?" the balding man asked as the train rumbled through the final leg of the journey to Rosslyn Station. Sarah Palmer exhaustedly tuned her ear to the conversation, trading brief glances with the man talking excitedly two rows ahead. He was speaking to two older gentlemen across from him, one a middle-aged man in colorful winter clothing, the other a grey-haired businessman. The bald man was also older but worn down, perhaps from the work he was now reflecting on. Sarah noticed that he was still in his work clothes: black Oxfords tied neatly over black socks, which rose to his tapered beige pants and light blue button-down. He was the caricature of an intellectual, but his Brooklyn accent bore another image. "Either I enjoy it now, or I die and someone else enjoys it. And what's the point of that?" he urged, glancing back and forth between his two companions. Sarah had a feeling they were all strangers, bound together by one man's passion and a D.C. train.

"I feel like I'm married to my job," the businessman said tiredly. "The last time I took a two-week vacation, I felt guilty." The colorful man nodded eagerly and sighed "yeah, yeah," pulling at the fabric on his multi-hued gloves.

"That's what I'm saying!" the bald man chimed in again. "Why spend your whole life earning money for someone else to enjoy it?"

Just then the train started to slow as Rosslyn Station slid into view like a slideshow reel. Sarah gathered her belongings and stood up from her seat. Steadying her balance as the train came to a stop, she stole one last glance at the three men; undoubtedly, the bald man was leading the charge, the other two his captive audience as he grew flush hot with the ardor of his words. She smiled to herself at the unlikely appearance of this newly-bred leader and walked off the train.

The cold blast of crisp air livened her nerves and quickened her pace down the steps of the platform. As she walked home, she began to ponder the words she had heard spoken by the bald man. She liked her job as Office Assistant at the Center for Global Development, but it wasn't what she'd always wanted. In spite of having a well-paid job and almost three degrees, she felt stagnant. The sacrifices we make to give up our dreams are often greater and more painful than the ones we make to achieve them.

# Dialog Vignette between Maya and Daphne

"It's not the side effects of the cocaine; I'm thinking that it must be love. It's too---"

"---OK. No," Maya says as she ejects her daughter's tape from the cassette player.

"Mom."

"Mom, what?"

"You said I could play anything I wanted. Isn't that what you said?"

"I did say play what you want. I did. I didn't know you'd play that. Cocaine…cocaine side effects? What? That's what you listen to?"

"I thought you liked David Bowie?"

"Yeah, sure. Like, let's dance David Bowie."

"_"

"-I can't believe they let you listen to that stuff in there."

"Let me?"

"Not let you. But…permit you."

"Permit me?"

"You know what I mean."

"You act like I was in a detention center or something. I wasn't in captivity."

"Please don't get dramatic Daphne, not today. Please. It's Thanksgiving, let's be thankful."

"I'm not being dramatic. I'm really not. And I am thankful. Thankful for David Bowie for once. Really mom, I'm just tired of your little…narrative."

"What narrative?"

"That I was in some sorta jail for a year or something. It was rehab. I was getting better. Rehab. Not exactly fucking Guantanamo."

"Don't curse."

"I didn't mean to. It's just---"

"---I know---"

"---No you don't. You really do not know. If you did know, I wouldn't be fucking cursing at you right now, but you don't know so I am."

"You better change your attitude fast. We're almost at your aunt's house."

"You better change your attitude fast. We're almost at your aunt's house," Daphne repeats at her mother, mocking her mom's very Boston accent.

"You're not funny," her mother says hiding a well-earned smile.

"To be hateful."

"What?"

"The Bowie song? It's too late to be grateful. It's too late to be late again. It's too late to be hateful."

"Oh. Hm."

"So what do you think?"

"About what?"

"About the song? The David Bow---"

"---Hey, we're here. Let's go. Button up your sweater. Be nice to your little cousins this time."

# Vinny: Vignette 1

8:30 pm. Vinny stood in the kitchen preparing his dinner, the same as every night: two sausages, one piece of black bread, one egg. Mindlessly, he arranged the ingredients on a plate and sat down at the kitchen table. He ate in silence, unthinking, playing out the routine that was one of many fixtures in his daily life. After dinner, he would prepare for bed and be asleep by 9:30; sometimes, 10 if his mind wandered too much. Tonight, however, his routine would be broken. Just as he'd finished his meal, the phone rang. He glanced at the caller ID: Elias. He picked up.

"I'm guessing it's important," Vinny said coolly. Elias didn't call this late unless it was urgent.

"It is. It really is. I found something - well, someone - I don't know, it's - I -"

"Spit it out, man," Vinny barked.

"Do you have a son?"

Vinny paused. He sat back in his chair and closed his eyes, pinching the bridge of his nose between his fingers. "There's no way," he thought.

"Hello? Vinny?" Elias called from the other end.

"Yeah, I'm here," Vinny breathed. "You need to come over, Elias. And bring everything you've found."

"Yes, okay, sure, I'll be right over. Um, bye."

"Bye." Vinny hung up the phone and slid it down the table, away from him. He slumped down further in his chair and threw his head back, rubbing his eyes. After resting there for a minute, he got up, picked up his dinner plate, and walked to the sink. As he waited for Elias, he moved on with his nightly routine. Tonight would be a night his mind would wander.

# Maya: Vignette 2

Tomorrow I'll wake up like a billion bucks. I'll feel like a woman that men want. I'll be able to walk up to any man and he will fall to his knees and say: "Tell me what you want me to do. And so it shall be done."

Tomorrow he will not say no.

*4:25 AM*

Platform. Subway. Platform. Dupont Circle. Starbucks. Studio.

*5:17 AM*

Walking into my gym, I whipped my hair up into a ponytail and greeted all my waiting students with a smile. We are playing pretend. They're pretending to not be Machiavellian dark lord Masters of the Universe and I'm pretending that they have souls.

They're all here. Only because it's Monday. By Wednesday, only half will be here. By Friday, it'll just be me, three middle-aged housewives, and him. Wait…where is he?

*5:24:56 AM*

I'm pretending to not be anxiously watching the LED gym clock when he finally strolls in and blesses me with his cool voice: "Maya."

Not hello, not how are you, not sorry I'm the only thing on your mind. Ever. Nope. Just…Maya.

I smiled and nodded back and smiled harder and started to say Hello, but no words left my mouth so I just start the class and stop trying to do talking things with my mouth.

*6 AM*

*Buzzer. Final stretch. Pointless conversation. Shower. Makeup.*

*6:13 AM*

The cleaning lady is here but, because of gender roles, she must wait another 5 or 10 minutes for the ladies' locker room to empty out. Of course, because of poor hygiene, the men's locker room has already been emptied.

Except for him. Where is he?

*6:37 AM*

The cleaning lady throws up her arms and apologizes, she really must go, she has other gyms nearby with less understanding managers. I understand and see her out.

What's he doing in there?

*6:58 AM*

My blood is hot and my heart is exploding. The sensation of terror.

I suddenly realized something must be wrong, terribly wrong. He's in danger. He is hurt. He is in pain. It's too late.

Something is wrong. Something must be wrong.

I rushed to the men's locker room and pressed my ear against the door I should never enter. Before I can open the door, the door is opened on me.

"Maya?"

He stretched his long arm down to help me up off the floor but I don't need him to get me up. He looked at me, looked at the door, then looked at me again. Before I could explain my sad self, he told me he has to meet his girlfriend for an early breakfast. He told me this in as few words as possible. Then he's gone.

Then I did something for no reason.

Though I wasn't in pain, I reached down and massaged my ring finger. I noticed the imprint on my flesh left from years of wearing my wedding ring. Then I kissed my branded finger.

I locked up and started my day.

# Sarah Palmer: Vignette 2

On the day she met Elias, the sky looked hazy and forlorn. Campus was quiet as she crossed Copley Lawn, her face buried in her phone. "I can't believe this," she murmured aloud, walking swiftly toward the library.

"Excuse me?" a voice called out. Sarah ignored it and kept walking; she was too busy trying to make sense of the e-mail she'd just received.

"Excuse me?" the voice tried again, louder this time. Sarah reluctantly stopped and looked up. She was met with a plain-faced boy of her height, whose face held a confused but endearing expression.

"Yes?" she replied, drily.

"Where can I find Copley Hall?"

He was standing right in front of it.

Sarah pointed irritably to her left, and the boy's eyes followed her finger.

"Ah, yes, I see," he smirked, "I've never been good with a map, you know?"

As he held her gaze, his expression became concerned. "Is everything okay?" he asked.

She averted her eyes. "I'm fine," she mumbled.

The boy seemed to pause for a second, then he perked up. "Hi, fine, I'm Elias!" he said cheerily, extending his hand out to her.

Sarah smiled faintly and shook his hand. "Haha, very funny."

"I tried," he replied. "Can I walk with you to wherever you're going?"

"I thought you were going to Copley Hall," Sarah said.

Elias shrugged. "It can wait."

# Daphne: Vignette 2

OnlineHost: ***You are in "Arts and Entertainment - Dead Kennedys". ***

OnlineHost: Welcome to the Plastic Surgery Disasters Forum

OnlineHost: 24 Dead Kennedys present. 23 active.

DaphneFrankenchrist1981: YT?

OnlineHost: EastBayR4yR4y has joined the chat.

OnlineHost: 25 Kennedys present. 23 active.

DaphneFrankenchrist1981: You have perfect timing.

EastBayR4yR4y: Been waiting long?

DaphneFrankenchrist1981: Only all day. But you already knew that <3

EastBayR4yR4y: I'm flattered

EastBayR4yR4y: Sup

DaphneFrankenchrist1981: nm

DaphneFrankenchrist1981: I lied. a lot going on

DaphneFrankenchrist1981: you like it, don't u?

EastBayR4yR4y: lol like what?????

DaphneFrankenchrist1981: you know…. Knowing that I'm excited to see u

EastBayR4yR4y: oh come on

DaphneFrankenchrist1981: I'm gonna ask you one more time

DaphneFrankenchrist1981: asl

EastBayR4yR4y: ….

EastBayR4yR4y: do you have a bf?

DaphneFrankenchrist1981: why do u think I'm a girl?

EastBayR4yR4y: DAPHNEFrankenchrist1981

DaphneFrankenchrist1981: HAHAHAHAHAHAHAHAHHHHH

DaphneFrankenchrist1981: why do u care if I have a bf?

EastBayR4yR4y: does he like the Kennedys?

DaphneFrankenchrist1981: 9

DaphneFrankenchrist1981: brb

EastBayR4yR4y: g2g

DaphneFrankenchrist1981: wait

**OnlineHost: EastBayR4yR4y has left the chat**

**OnlineHost: 24 Kennedys present. 23 active.**

***

When Daphne's online date pulls into the driveway, she is home alone. She hears the tires scoff the driveway but decides to register the sound as someone needing to make a U-turn. It's obvious someone with something to do and somewhere to be made a wrong turn and ended up in her cul-de-sac where nothing ever happens. Now they need to leave.

When Daphne's date knocks on the door, she loses her breath. It's really happening. She feels something rushing through her veins like the drugs used to—except this time around, it's not dopamine, its cortisol. She can only think one thing: *How do I cancel?*

She turns off all the lights in her room and holds her breath. After a few moments of silence, the knocking persists. Knowing that neither her mother nor Elias is home, she drags herself to their rooms anyway hoping that either of them would know how to handle this situation.

Of course, no one is home. She stands at the top of the stairs alone, watching the front door as it vibrates with the rhythm of her date's knocks. She only has two thoughts:

*I've brought this strange man to me and now what?*